Horses Can Roll but They Can't Roller Skate

JADE LEAHY

Illustrated by Julie Hollinshead

In aid of
Riding for the Disabled Association

Published by
The Author

Design & repro Mike Starkey

ISBN 978-1-5272-7959-9

Printed in England

Dedication

For Odin, my golden horse with a golden heart.

Acknowledgements

I would like to give special thanks to:

Sarah Lloyd Harris of The Stella Hayward Riding for The Disabled Association for her knowledge kindness and patience teaching me and Rosie.

Julie Holllinshead of Paint Paws for gifting delightful illustrations

Stephanie Darnill and Jo Hadfield for proof reading and editing

Karen Clithero of Crafty Ponies for her collaborative support

Mike Starkey for the design and repro

"I loved reading Jade's story, it's a heart-warming tale and shows challenges and diversity through the book, it took me back to my childhood riding days! A great read for children and a wonderful bedtime story"

Hannah Russell

Introduction

I created Molly and Odin's adventure several years ago and dismissed the idea of turning it into a children's book as a silly idea, who was I to publish a children's book?

Having lost Odin in 2018 I am embarking on a new journey with my cob Rosie, with the support of Sarah Lloyd Harris and the Riding for The Disabled Association. Publishing Molly and Odin's adventure is a fitting thank you to my beautiful Fjord horse and a way to give something back to The Riding for The Disabled Association, because every copy sold enables a donation.

I hope my inclusive children's book will encourage a positive attitude towards difference and a 'can do attitude' in children who face a variety of challenges.

Above all, I hope Molly and Odin's adventure will spread a little joy and that readers will love him as much as I did.

Jade Leahy

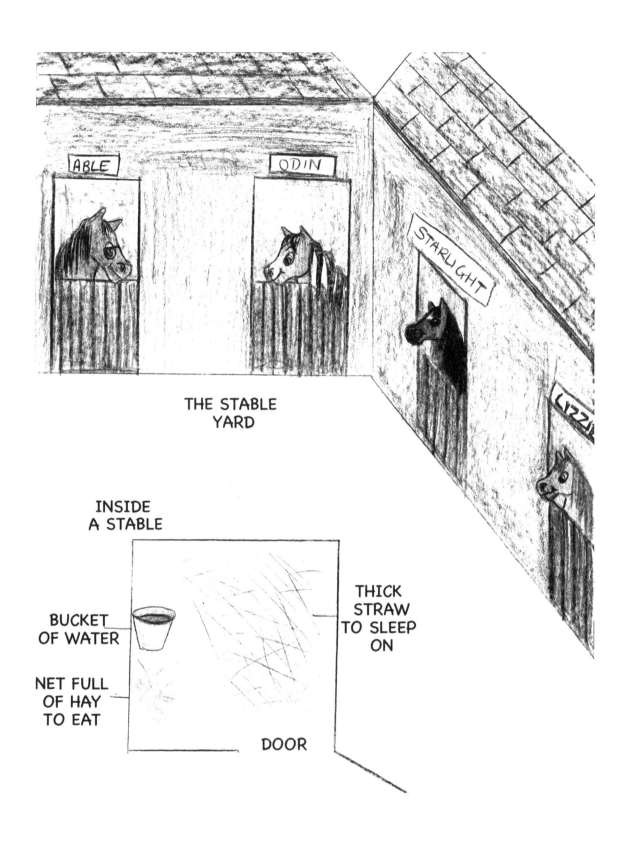

THE STABLE
YARD

INSIDE
A STABLE

BUCKET
OF WATER

NET FULL
OF HAY
TO EAT

THICK
STRAW
TO SLEEP
ON

DOOR

Home Sweet Home

Able, the old police horse, mostly kept himself to himself – or at least he tried to.

He had a nosy neighbour, you see. 'Whatshisname' the little Fjord horse, was forever stretching his head over the wall at Rest-A-While stables and tuning in with his 'listening ear'.

At that moment the little Fjord horse (or Odin, that's his real name) was comfortably resting his bottom on the hay rack, waiting for Able to begin telling him his story.

If he'd glanced up he'd have noticed that even the spiders who lived in the top corners of the stable were sitting in their webs, waiting for Able to begin his story too. Odin was a bit frightened of spiders so he never looked up at the corners of the stable.

Odin's stable was in the centre of the stable block and despite the cobwebs in the corners, it was 'Home Sweet Home'.

He had his own fluffy bed, his own water bucket, hay rack and feed bowl in the lefthand corner which was filled with a dinner ration every day at 5.30pm.

The dinner was too small in Odin's opinion. If the stable girls were serving the evening meal all of the 'dinnerguests' neighed loudly or snorted to tell them off!

'Home Sweet Home' was airy, Odin had his stable door open with a chain across the doorway in the daytime and swallows would dive in and out as they gathered bits of hay and straw for their nests.

Odin and the swallows were all sitting comfortably, so Able began telling his Home Sweet Home story.

Odin had heard his stories many times but he always wanted to hear them again. He looked up to Able because he was brave, but also because he was a huge 16 hand horse. He probably used to be very muscley, but now he was a little bit bony because he was getting old. Able used to work for the police, dealing with all sorts of trouble. He used to work on busy city streets with his policeman owner, Bobby.

"Horses here don't know they're born," said Able. "During my police days, I battled through seas of angry people, chairs, bricks, bottles came flying through the air, sometimes they would hit me and although I was scared I had to hold in my fear and I'd battle on, pushing past the crowds as they fought each other.

There was screaming, shouting, smashing, as the things they threw flew past my face, but I wore a shield."

"Cool," said Odin, amazed. Bobby was a real-life warrior, "Can we see the medals?" he asked. Odin loved this bit.

Able stretched up to the small box in the corner and nudged it. Out dropped two dusty old medals that probably used to be really shiny, the Blue Cross medal and the Dicken medal.

"A real life hero," thought Odin.

Able said: "Once a year Bobby and I would show people the sort of things we did every day. We would take part in a show that humans seemed to love. The other police horses and I would show them how we rode through fire, and how brave we were."

Sometimes Able still had nightmares but he didn't want the youngster to know about all that.

Odin couldn't imagine how Able could be so brave.

"He's really someone, a hero," thought Odin. Odin dreamt of fame. One day he'd be someone too! His great aunt had always said that, and she was right.

Odin's ancestors were Viking horses and his mum, Maple Dagmar and his dad Ausdan Otto, were very well bred.

Odin had been born with a pigeon toe; his right toe turned inward. His mum always said he was perfectly imperfect.

He wasn't perfect and that's how he ended up at Rest-A-While stables. Odin did riding lessons. He trudged along looking like Eeyore from Winnie the Pooh as impatient children yanked him around the ring, kicking their legs with all their might to make him go.

His ears were almost flat against his head, he was unhappy.

Odin remembered what his aunt had said. She was right, he was definitely cut out for stardom and he'd even been practicing his hoof print! Imagine the serpentines (those figure of eight moves that all the famous horses do) he'd mix in when he was famous...

But Odin wasn't a someone. He wasn't like the school horses or the pony club ponies. All the 'someones' were bay (that's posh for brown). Odin was a Fjord horse – grubby, sandy yellow with a brown donkey stripe down his back and a big bushy black and white zebra mane.

Boy oh boy, he longed to be a brown horse and do mounted pony club games with the 'in gang'! But how could you be in their gang when you were scared of Hissing Sid? Odin was terrified of Hissing Sid. Hissing Sid didn't always come to life.

Sometimes he was coiled, sometimes he was loose across the yard or the edge of the field.

This morning the stable girl Izzy, was leading Odin back from the 'fatties' field', (too much grass could make chubby ponies chubbier, so ponies who were already chubby had to graze in the field that didn't have too much grass in it and it was known as 'the fatties field').

He was hoping there was a nice breakfast in his stable, when he saw Hissing Sid stretched out across the yard.

He held his breath and tiptoed past him, trying not to make a sound.

Just as he let out a sigh of relief, Hissing Sid sprang to life, a hissing woosh sound, and then Sid started moving.

Odin couldn't be brave like Able, he jumped as Hissing Sid made a noise and gushed out water. They began a sort of ballet dance as Odin moved from one foot to the other, trying to get as far away from Sid as quickly as he could. His eyes got wider as green Hissing Sid snaked closer.

In the end he was so scared that he spun round as fast as he could, twirling the stable girl round so quickly that her feet came off the ground, as she pirouetted and almost went up in the air. He trotted back to his stable at high speed and hid behind his door.

When he dared to peep out Hissing Sid had stopped gushing water and was asleep again.

The stable girl could never understand why Odin was scared of something as harmless as a hosepipe.

A Race With Starlight

Safe in his stable and safe from Hissing Sid, Odin looked over at the gang on the other side of the yard. The 'in gang' were the pony clubbers.

The Pony Club ponies did lessons once or twice a week. They were fit, like mini athletes. They had toned muscles, and coats so shiny you could see your face in them because the Pony Club team spent so much time grooming them.

Odin, on the other hand, had such a big bushy mane. Sometimes birds used to pull his hair to line their nests with it and make them warm and comfy. He was always dreaming about being one of those shiny, bay ponies. He ached to join their club and take part in their activities. "It sounds amazing," mused Odin.

"They do all sorts, dressage, polo and mounted games." (Mounted games involved riders racing their ponies in teams weaving in and out of poles and cones, relay races and all sorts of fun).

He had only ever heard stories about the Pony Club Championships as no one from their stables had ever made the grade. He wished with his whole heart that he could make the grade. Odin was sure that another horse, Starlight, would make it. He used to watch him and his rider practicing in the school, trotting over the wooden poles lined up for ponies and their riders to trot over.

Starlight could do anything and was so glamorous! He was another of Odin's heroes, a Pony Club pony and bound to become as famous as Seabiscuit, a famous racehorse that everyone had heard of and he was so fast they'd made films about him. Starlight was a shiny bay pony with four perfect white socks and a perfect white star in the middle of his forehead (which was probably why he was called Starlight when he was born). Even his brow band was sparkly...

Odin's was just scuffed and plain. Odin didn't ever get to do pony racing or mounted games, not even the stable events, let alone Pony Club events. Apparently, he wasn't 'that sort of horse'.

Every Wednesday evening, he prayed that he might get tacked up for the Pony Club lesson. No matter how hard he scrunched his eyes up and wished, as he munched his hay, he never did although he had managed to make a hole in his net so he could chomp much more hay much more quickly – result!

This morning however, he had the chance to have a race. Odin and Starlight were put in the sand school whilst their stables were cleaned out. The sand school was like a large square field filled with sand instead of grass. It had trotting poles and jumps laid out with letter markers on the fence. Odin didn't like school at all, but this morning was different because they weren't doing lessons, they were loose.

Odin and Starlight lined up at the fence by the far side. Odin made himself as tall as he could and gave Starlight a winner's stare. With their noses level, Starlight snorted and on the count of three, they were off – 1, 2, 3...

Odin ran as fast as he could halfway around the school and they were neck and neck. He was racing a hero and he, Odin Fjord, was winning. He was a whisker ahead but as they got to the 'S' marker next to the horse walker, (which was like a giant hamster wheel for horses), Starlight galloped past. Odin tried as hard as he could, stretching his neck right out to try and catch up with Starlight, but it was no good. He just wasn't good enough; he wasn't a winner.

Ah well, he'd keep dreaming and hoping and wishing.

Bethany Seabiscuit and Lizzie

His dreams weren't going to come true this Sunday either. Odin was saddled with the beginners' lessons – the Sunday morning bunch of raggle-taggle ponies charged with ambling slowly around while youngsters yanked inexpertly on their reins.

The Sunday Bunch consisted mainly of children who didn't really seem to be very good at riding. He usually ended up with 'BETHANEEEY' (as he called her because that's the way her mum squealed her name with delight as they bounced around the ring). Bethany's mother was expecting her to move up to the Pony Club group. "Poor them," thought Odin.

Bethany was about nine years old, very short, very fat and very spoilt. She had a square bob with a thick fringe which only made her face seem even rounder.

Every time she arrived at the stables, she stomped her way from her mum's Citroën to the mounting block in her jodhpurs. She was always in a bad temper because she wanted another packet of sweets.

Odin dreaded his lessons. Bethany banged up and down on his back and kicked his sides again and again to make him trot faster and faster, until he was bruised and scowling under his forelock. What was the point? Neither of them would ever make the Pony Club set if he couldn't even win a race!

Odin turned his thoughts to happier things – Seabiscuit, an incredible American

Bethaneeeeey!

racehorse, and another of Odin's heroes. He adored Seabiscuit. If they could just chat, he was sure they would become the best of friends. Seabiscuit was a legend, just like Starlight he was a winner!

Odin had only found out about Seabiscuit because one of the pony clubbers stuck a poster of him on Odin's stable wall and chuckled repeatedly as she sellotaped it fast. Odin often wondered whether Seabiscuit had ever had to do Pony Club or a 'Sunday Bunch' – somehow he doubted it... Odin thought about how he could make himself more like Seabiscuit.

However, much Odin idolised Seabiscuit, his devotion paled beside his own fan club of one, Lizzie the logging pony. Lizzie was a small, flea-bitten, grey Welsh cob – (that means she had freckles rather than itchy fleas). She looked like a unicorn minus the horn, but there was definitely some Welsh dragon in her!

She was only a little lady, but she was stubborn and strong. She often pulled an old cart that was used to collect logs. Wherever Odin went, Lizzie wasn't far behind. This morning it was no different. The little sandy Fjord horse rolled his eyes in disgust when he realised that Lizzie had crept in to listen to Able's story too.

Odin always tried to hide whenever he heard Lizzie coming. It was hard to hear her when she wasn't harnessed to her cart. He dreaded the high-pitched squeaking of her old cart, which was very bent and buckled.

Lizzie adored Odin even more than she loved mints. She was always trying to stand next to him and snuggle, but it made Odin want to puke - well, he would have puked if horses could be sick. She loved Odin even though he was in part responsible for the damage to her cart.

Odin had been trudging round in the sand school with one of the Sunday bunch, when he heard the sound he dreaded, 'squeak, squeak, squeaky, squeak', which meant Lizzie was nearby. He pretended not to hear her or her cart. He was busy.

All at once, before he could do anything, Lizzie Logger charged towards the sand school and jumped clean over the fence, dragging her little cart behind her, just like the cow who jumped over the moon, in the old nursery rhyme.

She ran towards Odin. He picked up speed but the quicker he ran, the quicker Lizzie and her cart followed. Odin ran faster than he ever had with the Sunday bunch. It was his worst nightmare: Lizzie logger chasing him. Lizzie was fine but her cart was a bit bent and buckled. Odin began to feel tearful and wished his life was different.

Molly

Just at the same time, someone else was wishing things were different too: a little girl called Molly.

Molly was nine-and-a-half years old and was a pupil at St Bartholomew's Primary School in the next village. She was in the A set for maths and French and the B set for science, so she was pretty smart. She sort of liked school, and maths was her favourite lesson, but the school uniform was horrible.

The winter uniform was a tartan kilt, beige shirt and tartan tie, with a disgusting bottle green blazer and pork pie hat (yuk). Still, at least they had a third break in the afternoon.

Molly had a few friends at school but her best friend would always be Penny. Penny was the opposite of Molly – tall, skinny and very sporty with a mop of blonde girly hair that always went frizzy in the rain. She always won the sprint race and loved tennis lessons. She was also really good fun and loved playing tricks on people.

Molly was quite short with greenish grey eyes and long, stick-straight fair hair. Penny wanted straight hair and Molly longed for curls, so Molly would straighten Penny's hair and Penny would spend ages curling Molly's.

Molly and Penny had been friends since the very first day of playschool. They were completely different, but both loved make-up. They were such good

friends that Penny always picked Molly to be her partner in the three-legged race at the school sports day. They came last every year, because Molly couldn't run. They fell over three times this year, but Penny didn't seem to care. She loved Molly more than winning a prize at sports day.

Molly was sitting at home, looking out of the window at the park opposite her houses, longing to be out with everyone. Her eyes prickled as she fought back tears and tried to get on with her homework.

It was no use – eventually a single tear made the ink of her last long division run. She scribbled it out and started again. She scribbled so hard she bent the nib of her fountain pen. She would probably get told off for using a ballpoint pen again, but she didn't care.

Even though she knew it was pointless, she still longed for roller skates. She abandoned her homework and forced herself to watch the other children skating round and round the outside of the park. It made her feel so sad she felt a pain in her insides, a hole in her soul.

Some kids had inline skates, some kids had quad skates. Penny had retro quad skates, blue ones with rainbow stripes. Any skates would have made Molly the happiest girl in the world!

Molly couldn't have skates because there had a been an accident when she was very little and she couldn't walk properly; some of her muscles were weak and painful. Every Wednesday, after school she had to have physio, to stretch out her muscles and improve her balance. She was supposed to do a balancing exercise and stretches at home but she could only really be bothered to do the ones that could be done whilst watching TV in her room. What was the point, as she couldn't roller-skate or do ballet?

Molly was wobbly when she walked and had to use a wheelchair for longer distances. She hated the wheelchair more than anything and she thought it was hideous and ugly.

She didn't even feel like a real person – it made her feel like a robot. None of her friends needed a chair. The chair was most definitely not cool, it was embarrassing. She often wondered why life was so unfair.

Skates were cool, and she would jolly well have some.

She was jolted from her thoughts by her mother bellowing, "DINNER!" and she made her way to the table. She'd ask for skates again. Maybe someone could help her skate?

Penny had let her try out her skates, but Molly had fallen over and cut her head open before she'd barely begun to skate and that had led to a lot of trouble for both of them.

At the dinner table she decided to tackle her mother first.

Molly's mother was a tall, skinny, immaculate lady, constantly busy with various village activities and committees, church cleaning, the village fete, neighbourhood watch. She had grown tired of explaining that skates were too unsafe for Molly and skating was too hard for her to be fun. Molly argued back, saying that piano was hard, but she was still made to play the stupid thing.

Her mother had insisted that Molly had piano lessons and her mother was having lessons as well. Molly scowled as they took it in turns to bash out the same pieces on the old wooden piano.

Everything she played sounded out of tune on it. Molly wasn't sure if it was the secondhand piano or their musical skills that were to blame.

Her mum just didn't understand how skates mattered to her, so as the dinner was served, she decided to try her dad, using different tactics. First, she brought up how well she had done in the school maths test. Then she steered the conversation round to a reward... She told her dad the only thing she was desperate for was SKATES - retro, inline, any kind of skates. Lunchtimes would be ace if she could put her skates on with her friends!

There was only one other girl that didn't have skates, Bethany. Bethany was into ponies and stuff. She spent lunchtimes reading her Pony Magazine and she didn't even have a stupid pony either.

Molly was more desperate for skates than anything, more desperate than she had been for an iPhone. She had wanted an iPhone because everyone else in the years above had one. But the only person she would have called was Penny.

Penny lived with her mum on the other side of the village. Penny had an iPhone too. She had most things girls her age didn't have because her dad bought her everything, even things she didn't really want. Penny's parents didn't live together anymore. Her dad lived with a girlfriend, who Penny hated, but she had to pretend to like because she loved her dad.

Molly enjoyed going to Penny's dad's house. Penny's dad let them do whatever they liked. Penny had bought glittery red hair spray and Molly took over her bright pink nail varnish and they spent hours singing on Penny's karaoke machine pretending they were on MTV. The red glittery spray turned Penny's white blonde ponytail a sickly pink colour.

When Penny got home, her mum went bananas and made her sleep with a plastic bag over her pillow. She grounded her for three weeks, which was awful as they were always meeting up after school and at the weekends. It was the longest three weeks ever as they could only see each other at break times.

Molly forced her attention back to her dad, who was looking distinctly nervous at her insistence on a set of skates. "Look," he pleaded. "We said that we would get you a little puppy. Imagine – a little bundle of fluff! I bet all your friends would love a bouncy little Jack Russell puppy."

Molly's dad was quite different to Molly's mum. Her dad didn't get involved in any village activities. He was a tall, thin man with a friendly face. He was quietly spoken and constantly worried. He did something important in an office.

He always carried a briefcase and had a variety of different coloured waistcoats for work. Molly didn't even know exactly what he did. When he tried to explain it, it sounded boring and she lost interest.

"Don't you get it? I don't WANT a stupid puppy. I just want the skaaaates!" Molly screeched.

Molly ate the rest of her meal in silence. Her mum's gravy seemed lumpier than usual. She didn't want a puppy because every other dog the family had, had pulled her over, although she did still love dogs.

Molly's dad looked awkward and his eye twitched through the rest of dinner. She'd noticed his eye always twitched if he was stressed or nervous. Molly's mother made his eye twitch a lot!

Odin's Bad Day

A few Sundays later, Odin was feeling particularly confused. He had got his hopes up! He hadn't been tacked up for the 'Sunday Bunch' as usual, something quite different had happened. He had been taken to the local show.

Had they seen his potential..? He knew it had to happen... he was off to do Pony Club games! Wowsers!!!!! Maybe he was off to the Pony Club championship?

His dreams were going to come true, he would be a star... What if he got chosen to do the relay! One day he might even race like Seabiscuit – imagine!

He would have his name embroidered on a numnah in gold letters, (in other words a really posh blanket to go under his saddle). How would he cope with being recognised? Did fame bring larger dinners? How would the other horses treat him when he was a star? If he was going to be a four-star horse, he wanted the lifestyle, thank you very much, including better accommodation!

He would probably get Able's stable, which was roomier and had a larger hay net.

He squealed with delight and practically pranced into the horse box. When Odin was led off the trailer, he gasped as he saw the sign in the arena – 'Gymkhana'. This was what the pony clubbers did! Maybe I could graze with the bays if I were an 'honorary brown', he thought. Woohoo! He felt like doing a little canter of happiness! Then his imagination began to run riot. Oh my, he thought, imagine if I made it to the Championship – his tummy turned into a mass of butterflies.

Odin stood still as a statue as he waited to be brushed and plaited, ready to admire his own face in the mirror. But he started to worry because they seemed to be getting clothes out for him... some kind of a hat – oh dear!

Mind you, he had always been told that he was related to warrior horses. Norwiegan Fjords, were an ancient breed.

'Odin' was the name of the Norse God of war and wisdom. He often imagined himself in a Viking hat. He definitely didn't think he was brave enough for a battle though, Hissing Sid was scary enough.

This didn't look the sort of hat worn by brave steeds..."Oh crumbs," he thought. His heart sank, and he let out a sigh. His pony club dream came crashing around his ears.

He wasn't wearing a warrior outfit; they were turning him into a flower! His rug was made of a fuzzy green material (very, VERY itchy) and he was wearing a hat fashioned into a great big daisy! A little tiny rider was put on his back, dressed as a fairy.

He didn't feel 'canter-happy' now. He really hoped there were no cameras to capture his shame. He hoped he didn't see anyone he knew. Imagine if this got back to the Pony Club browns! Good stuff just didn't happen to him. "Being bay is cool; stripy is definitely not cool," he thought."

He doubted Seabiscuit had ever had to dress up as a flower, or any kind of plant. Oh WHY hadn't they picked stupid old Daisy Moo, the black and white piebald. She could have come as a cow; she was black and white, and she wouldn't even have had to dress up! Still at least the fairy they put on top of him was tiny...

Odin had a big, black cloud over his head.

Molly's Bad Day

Molly was having a bad day too. Her parents announced that they had a special surprise planned... Molly's heart sank.

It was a Sunday, so it definitely wasn't shopping for skates. Oh no, it was probably shopping for puppy stuff. She'd rather stay at home! I mean it's not like she didn't love dogs but she didn't want a pet that pulled her over and her friends loved skating.

Molly sighed and got in the car. Her dream of a pair of skates was looking very far away now. Her heart sank even further into her boots when they pulled up at some horse riding stables.

Oh no – even worse, thought Molly. They had brought her to brush a pony, while everyone else rode them. How thoughtful – NOT. She couldn't even ride a pony so certainly didn't want to watch other people have fun with them. A horse bit her once in the New Forest. "At least puppies are cuddly," she thought to herself.

Molly's parents knew that horse riding would be good for her muscles and would help her to walk.

Her dad lugged her chair out of the car. She'd need it as the ground was uneven and her dad didn't want her to fall over. Just then – "Oh no!" She spied at least two girls from school: weird Bethany and someone from the year above... She could have died of embarrassment – they couldn't miss her in the wheelchair.

Dad asked Molly if she wanted to meet the horse... she totally didn't. There was a cute mini one and the riders looked as if they were having fun, but she really wasn't up for watching other people do fun stuff again. "No," she snapped, and chewed on another Haribo. They said they'd bring the pony out for her to meet it. She was sure the pony flared its nostrils as they told it she was here.

When the instructor said she would go and get the pony to meet Molly, Odin was hugely insulted. "Pony indeed – I AM A HORSE!!" he wanted to cry." "With IMPORTANT ancestors!"

But he just snorted in disgust and put his bum to the door. "If I could have, I would have said talk to the hoof," he thought to himself. He often practiced singing into a carrot too.

He shuddered when he thought of his floral bonnet. Then he shook himself and remembered that he had visitors. And visitors often meant FOOD. "I'll just let out a little whinny in case the humans have brought any of those little mints with the hole that I absolutely love - yummy!" thought Odin.

Izzy the stable girl dragged him to the front of the stable. Odin tried hard to force out a tummy rumble. He had learnt tummy rumbles made all humans feel sorry for ponies. "Extra yummies for me," thought Odin as his stomach roared like a lion.

He stuck his head out gingerly over the door. He could smell carrots. He could almost taste them, but he couldn't see them. He tried not to look too keen. "They might make me do more stuff with BETHANEEEY, ugh," he thought.

"I'm down here," Molly snapped. "You probably can't see me, sitting down as usual." Her dad put a pathetically sympathetic hand on her shoulder. "Riding will be good for your muscles Molly," said her dad. Molly thought: "Sometimes

I hate dad; I hate puppies and ponies and I HATE stupid skates!"

She tried to stretch to feed the carrot to the pony. It was different from the other ponies you see in magazines, kind of like a zebra – not the usual boring brown.

"Well, this was an interesting kind of human," thought Odin. "It isn't a 'two legs' but definitely a funny kind of 'four legs'... a human never has four, does it? It's far too short, anyway."

"Oh well," he thought. "It has food, and I can just about reach it. How lazy – she didn't even pass it to me. Still she was better than BETHANEEEY, all screechy in my face and squeezing me."

While Odin chewed the carrot the boss woman asked the small human if she'd like a ride. "Oh nooo," thought Odin, "another 'Sundayer', another bruise." He decided to switch off and just daydream about him and Seabiscuit becoming buddies.

It seemed to take the really small human even longer to climb on to his back than it took BETHANEEEY. thought Odin. At least she was lighter.

"... I wonder what kind of passengers Seabiscuit had in the early days?" he mused. "Before he made it big, when he was first doing lessons."

Odin waddled over to the sand school for another horrible half an hour. He wondered if his saddle was done up a bit tight as he could barely breathe. "I'm on half a hay ration!" he thought. "But what those smarty pants humans don't know is if I crane my neck, I can just reach far enough to steal seconds from the old boy next door. He forgets how much he had in his net anyway..."

He squeezed out a bottom burp. The bottom burp made the passenger chuckle. (A bottom burp is a squelchy one, a wind pop is a hissy one.) "Thank goodness she's laughing," he thought. "I thought she looked like a crier – phew!"

"Right, sit up tall and sit back," said the instructor, "and Odin will walk around with you. Smile and breathe! Well done!"

Molly was terrified, she couldn't smile or breathe and felt like crying. "Molly is definitely a wobbler, bouncing about like a yo-yo in the saddle," thought Odin. "But I kind of like her. She's quiet and doesn't bruise me... She actually gave me a lovely shoulder scratch too – ooh, it was so nice, it made my top lip curl right over."

"Well, I'm on board," thought Molly. Being put on the pony was pretty embarrassing, so she imagined herself rollerblading with Penny instead. They entered the ring..."

Molly's dad led the zebra horse and people walked by the side of her so that Molly felt safe. Although she was scared, the pony was comfy and he smelt nice, and he was sort of cool with his mad zebra mane.

Odin's half an hour went more quickly than usual, but his tummy was still rumbling. He licked and chewed as he tried to decide what he would change his name to if he became famous... like Seabiscuit.

"I'd probably change it to something...fast and chocolatey? The human, Molly – I must call her Molly because I hate it when people just call me 'the horse' or even worse, 'The PONY'. I think I like her, No yanking with the reins, but chomping chaff – she really could talk the hind leg off a donkey.

"Molly told me all about how this was a 'substitute hobby' because she couldn't have skates. I put my ears back. I am no substitute! I have a pedigree! I have no idea what skates are, but they seem to make her awfully sad."

He was just feeling gloomy about this, when he heard her say he must be sad because all horses probably dream of being Seabiscuit in their heads... "Oh my goodness!" he thought excitedly to himself. "She said Seabiscuit! She SAID, SEABISCUIT!"

He thought fast: "Maybe they are pen pals? Could Seabiscuit use a pen? Or would he have a groom to use it for him? Maybe Seabiscuit and Molly are friends?"

He broke into a spritely trot, resisting the urge to burst into one of his canters of happiness. She let out a 'yeeha' sound, which was encouraging, or was she scared? Molly was scared because trotting made her wobble. She asked to get off and her lesson ended.

Odin decided to tolerate her brushing him. He normally gave the other children a good nip (non-lesson time is eating time), but he put up with it in case she told him any more about Seabiscuit...

After Molly's Ride

"Well, that went well," Molly's dad said on the way home in the car.

Molly didn't reply. She didn't want to get over-enthusiastic about the whole thing, then she said: "I thought I was going to fall off!"

"But you didn't," said Molly's dad. "You looked great!"

"Did the stripy little barrel think we were playing cowboys and Indians? What if I had fallen off?" thought Molly to herself. "The Pony Club would have laughed at me, like the time I had to sit on my own in the dance lesson. And the time one of the boys wrote 'L for loser' on the inside of my desk and I felt like breaking his glasses..."

That evening Penny said she didn't feel like skating, so they went to the park. Penny chatted away about how much she hated ballet. Molly was starting to feel sad about ballet and skates, so she decided to mention the little zebra horse to Penny.

Penny instantly wanted to know every detail of how the lesson went, what the horse's name was, and what sort it was. Molly realised she had no idea what sort it was. She just knew it wasn't like the others; it wasn't plain brown...

Molly felt far more cheerful when Penny asked her all about the little horse and whether she could ride it too and they could learn together.

Thank goodness for the little zebra horse!

Molly and Penny usually ended up hatching the best plans for Penny to skive off her ballet exams. That was her dad's one strict rule: Penny had to do ballet lessons and she whinged her head off about it. It always made Molly feel dreadfully sad as she would have loved to have ballet lessons.

Most people in her class were dragged to ballet every Saturday morning. Molly usually had a lie-in on Saturday mornings and her mum always took her to Costa for a hot chocolate with marshmallows, but only after piano practice... YAWN.

Penny's ballet friends were all tremendously pretty and even wore their hair in a pretty bun to school. Molly often used to see some of them walking home from their class in their matching T-shirts, still with their leotards and wraparound cardigans on, because that's what you did in the 'in gang'.

Some of them even wore pink leg warmers now that 80s-style clothes were cool again...

Molly couldn't bear to watch as the happy gang wandered through town when she was with her mum... but she couldn't help watching them as they strolled along, fascinated by how their feet seemed to slightly turn out. She wondered if they did it on purpose or whether it was a habit formed from all the ballet lessons.

As Molly sat in the library the next day, she started thinking about the stables again. She counted down the days until Sunday and wondered what kind of other girls rode the little stripy horse during the rest of the week when she wasn't there.

Odin's Present

Whenever Odin was jealous or bored, hungry or tired – or any other feeling really, he became cheeky. Not nasty or unkind, just cheeky.

He'd finished his hay so craned his neck to try reaching the remaining three quarters of his elderly neighbour's net. As he munched away on his stolen hay Odin thought about his home at Rest-A-While Stables.

"Being a riding school horse was OK," he thought. "But it's not like being a family horse. Some of those family ponies have it made – stables like palaces, unlimited hay (or so they say). Mind you, an unlucky neddy had landed a home with BETHANEEEY's family..."

The poor little pony had been loaded into a shiny new lorry. The worst thing about Bethany other than Bethany in general, was Bethany's love of hugs, squeezy hugs...

Bruce was loaded into the lorry in a pink, sparkly head collar, pink, sparkly travel boots, a pink, sparkly rug and a pink tail guard. The pink grooming kit was tossed into the lorry with the pink, sparkly jumping whip and chubby Bethany hopped into the passenger seat in her brand -new, shocking pink jodhpurs.

Odin snorted sulkily: "Unlimited hugs too... Lucky, lucky Brucie!"

The lorry pulled away and Odin's head hung low as he was tacked up for the

HELP!

Brucie

Sunday class. He started to think about Seabiscuit and Starlight... had they had to do Sunday Bunch before they made it big?

He'd managed to suck the last few strands out of the hay net. Most unfortunately during the week, they'd replaced the net with a large hole for a new one without a handy hole.

Just as he popped a sprig of cow parsley into his mouth, he saw three humans in the distance. One seemed to be sitting... it was Molly. He served himself a second helping of cow parsley, pretending he hadn't noticed she'd arrived. He thought to himself: "Now I don't know a full conversation's worth of words, but I do know the most important ones like 'carrots', 'presents', ooh, and 'food'. I even know a couple of bad words like 'work' or 'school'."

He continued his munching, but felt a little tremor of excitement. "I definitely heard the word present," thought Odin excitedly. "Although that's not quite as good as food." He wondered if it was something he could eat?"

The humans approached, and he could see that it was neither food nor pink (poor Brucie). It was a shiny new saddle. He wasn't sure how he felt about this gift because it was most definitely a work-related gift.

"You'll be away now," the instructor said as she carefully placed the new saddle on the little Zebra Pony (sorry Odin, I mean HORSE).

Apparently, the saddle was a Western saddle just like a cowboy one. "Ooh, if Penny would give up the skating we could play cowboys and Indians like in the old movies," thought Molly. "Still, last week Penny grazed all the skin off her shin going downhill and scuffed her left skate, so she isn't quite so eager to skate after school, especially now her mum's forced her to wear a helmet."

Molly mused: "Odin stood as still as a statue whilst they lifted me on board. But I wanted to jump on and off like the girls in Bethany's riding magazine. I had a quick flick through Pony Magazine when she left it behind after third break. Oh well, we'll see how the zebra and I get on with the cowgirl saddle."

Horn to hold
on to
→

Seat to sit on
↓

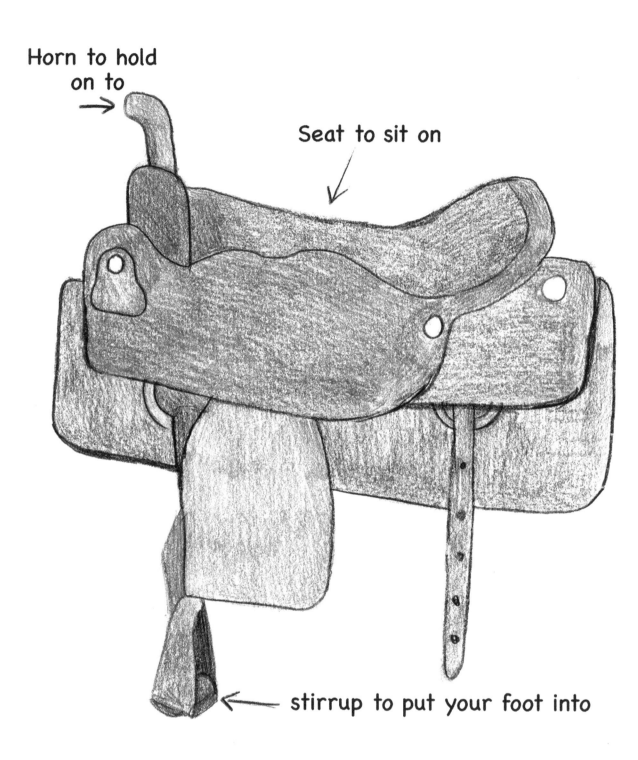

← stirrup to put your foot into

A quick adjustment to the stirrups, and the pair made their way into the school. Odin set off with Molly in the new Western saddle.

"Sit up tall", said the instructor. "Hold on to the horn of the saddle, so that you feel safe and give him a little tickle with the whip, so that he knows you are asking him to trot."

Molly felt nervous but decided to be brave. She tickled Odin's right hind leg with the whip, and he began a couple of strides of trot. Molly held on to the horn and up, down they began to trot. "I'm trotting, I'm trotting, I'm actually trotting!" cried Molly with delight. She had to admit the saddle was jolly comfy, and Odin seemed happy with it.

"I wonder if I should invest in my own hat," she thought. "I've got some money that I saved up for skating."

"At least Molly's lighter than Bethany," thought Odin. "She came last week for a lesson with Brucie, and he's wearing paint on his hooves now. Yep, pink paint!"

Molly became aware that the instructor had started to explain what she was going to do next. "Oooh golly," she thought. "Trotting poles? My legs are throbbing, I'm too tired, "And what if he jumps over it? I can't! Oh crikey, I want to cry, and my legs are shaking."

Odin had been really pleased with the lesson. It was quite fun, and best of all Molly got him out of doing the Sunday Bunch but as she started to sob in her saddle, he thought: "Oh no, a crier," and decided to stop.

He suddenly remembered that he had made a girl called Sophie cry in Sunday Bunch once. She had whinged all the way round that she was 'stuck with slow, boring Odin and she wanted to ride Starlight, the pony club pony'. "Huh – Starlight schmarlight", thought Odin.

His belly had been aching; earlier that morning he had eaten half an extra hay net and a load of lush grass because he had managed to limbo under the electric fence. He wanted the session to end, so he set off in his bounciest trot.

Her whinging got louder so he started to canter (not with happiness). Finally, he lost his temper and bucked Elspeth clean off. He got banned from Sunday Bunch for a while – oh well!

In her next lesson Molly felt ready for the poles. She held on to the horn and looked out over the arena, as she and Odin trotted merrily over the them, one at a time. "We did it, Check us out!" thought Molly, proudly. "We whizzed over them."

She nearly fell forwards but held on to the horn of the saddle Soon Molly and Odin were ready for another go, and another. Molly's confidence was starting to grow and she may even have enoyed it a little bit...

After the lesson Molly was bursting with pride and buzzing with happiness, and even dared to think about what she and her striped steed might do next. She imagined herself, jodhpurs on, hair in a bun as her name was called into the ring, "Competitor number 369 Molly Dillon on Odin." "Maybe she could learn to do an alternative form of ballet on Odin." She couldn't wait to tell Penny.

Molly and Odin

A month or so later, Molly had to think of a topic for a talk at school that week. She hated having to give talks at school, but this year was different. "I'm going to do my talk on Odin," she thought.

"I've got some information on his care and feed from the instructor and dad said he might even bring my saddle in to school. I took a load of pictures of him too. Odin seemed to quite like our photo shoot!"

Odin did indeed enjoy his photo shoot. The process of being groomed to a shine and made to pose for photographs made his heart swell with pride. It's a wonder his head was small enough to fit through his stable door.

"I, Odin, a horse, who is not brown, has found fame," he crowed. "Molly came and took lots of photos of me on her phone thing. Photos of me looking thoughtful with my head over my stable door (I borrowed Able's, I know it won't be long until I move in), photos of me being groomed, photos of me in the cow parsley, photos of me eating cow parsley; photos of me in my Wild West saddle.

"I want a star and lights around my stable door! Imagine if we make the paper. Imagine where this could lead... I might even feature in Pony Magazine!"

"The wait for Sundays seems like it takes forever," thought Molly with a sigh. "Almost like it's Christmas Eve all week.

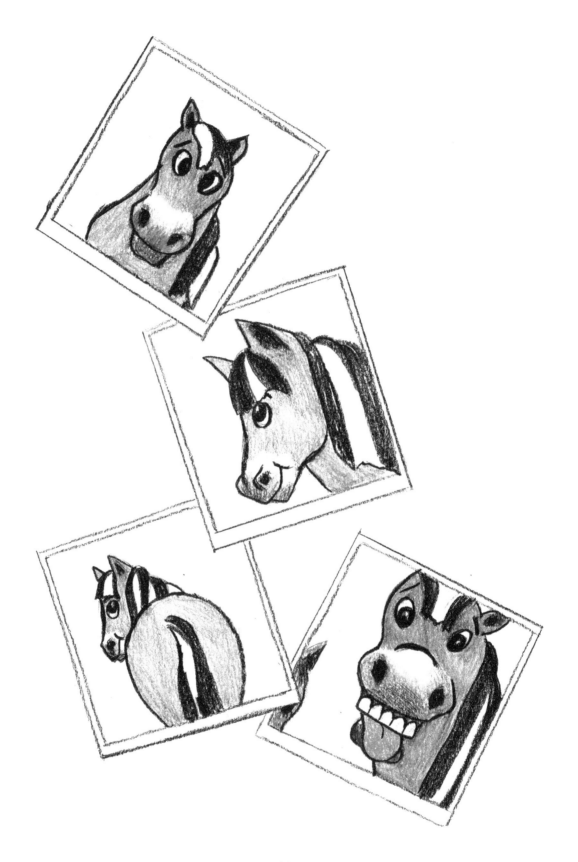

"My talk about Odin went really, really well. Everyone asked lots of questions about him and no one said anything awkward about me not being able to ride properly.

"Even weird Bethany asked a question; I felt sorry for her as everyone stared.

"Some of the girls from the Pony Club said we could meet up at the stable next week as they do Pony Club stuff there! Miss Clegg has even asked me to give a follow-up talk on how Odin and I are getting on with more photos of him. We might even be asked to do regular updates in the school magazine - there's no column for skaters, or for ballet dancers, so I feel smug!

"Thank goodness all this hasn't gone to Odin's head. I was so happy the talk went well that I have treated myself to a 'my own hat' and we are bound to be cantering soon."

These days after school Molly made sure that she did at least ten stretches on each leg and practiced her balancing, just in case it helped her ride better and improved her balance so that she could have fun with the Pony Club girls.

Odin resisted helping himself to some extra hay, in preparation for their first canter. He didn't want to be too heavy to perform gracefully.

"Right, use the horn to balance yourself and have a little canter, Molly," said her instructor. "Don't panic, Odin the wonder horse will look after you; just imagine you are on a rocking horse." Three strides was all they managed but they'd done three strides!

Odin thought, "Wonder horse – absolutely'! But rocking horse? I am definitely no rocking horse. They are dapple grey, and I have never had spots, ever!"

The extremely offended little horse thought: "My dad was a prize winner!" He was really quite good at dressage – which was a sort of horse ballet, his mum had told him.

He thought about bucking, but he loved Molly, so off he set like a rocking horse. He kept saying "rocking horse, rocking horse," over and over so that he remembered not to get too excited. Then Odin realised Molly was just as excited as he was. He paused and nodded his head up and down, before breaking into the most beautiful canter.

As gently as he could, he carried a frantically excited, pink-cheeked Molly on his back, who could hardly breathe through sheer joy and excitement. They were flying. A CANTER of happiness.

Molly was so happy, that it made Odin happy. For Molly, who had always struggled to walk any distance, it was thrilling to feel the rhythm of the little Fjord horse and hear the sound of his hooves on the ground even for a few minutes. Her heart felt like it would burst. She could ride! She could do whatever she wanted!

Molly: "Last week I went to the school disco with Penny and had the best time! I've had pictures of of flying Fjord horses put on the wheels of my chair. They were the talk of the school disco! No one has horses on their roller skates.

"We are unique! I even made friends with some of the 'in gang'. They've been watching me ride Odin and we are all going shopping on Saturday.

"Chelsea started chatting to me and said that Penny told her I ride, and she is totally desperate for a pony. She asked if she could come and see the one I ride. I told her I ride a HORSE!

"I left the disco early as it's a big day tomorrow, our first competition at the stables. Imagine if Odin and I became professional. How would I sign my autograph? What if someone knocks me over when I get mobbed? Oh, the camera flashes would hurt my eyes! Penny is coming to watch and may have lessons too so that we can learn together. I'm SO excited I could burst. I hope Odin is excited as well as hungry!

"We are competing in the riding school Pony Club games with the actual pony clubbers – wow. Chelsea has asked to be chief photographer and I'm taking my wheels as I might be a bit tired after our round. I think Odin is a bit nervous though. He bit a hole in my new jumper. It's just so unlike him."

"Wowsers," thought Odin... "I, a Fjord, who is not 'brown', will be competing in the riding school Pony Club competition. Seabiscuit, eat your heart out! I so want Molly and me to win. "I've been sneaking a bit of the big ex-race horse competition feed (called Speedi Mix) as I stroll past the feed room."

The Big Day

Several weeks later, the day of the competition arrived, and Elspeth and Starlight finished with a pole down and one refusal.

Next up were Molly and Odin, who were called into the ring. Molly looked smart in her new jodhpurs and hat. She felt sick with nerves. Odin felt sick because he snuck another mouthful of Speedi Mix from the feed room.

The bell rang and Odin let out a great big hiccup. (Pardon Odin. Still, it's better than a bottom burp from the other end!)

"Oh no – here comes my L for loser moment," thought Molly, but Odin set off like a little rocket! They cleared their first jump, and Molly whispered 'rocking horse' in his ear over and over again so that he remembered not to get over excited. They flew round the course with Odin's zebra mane and Molly's plaits flying behind them. She had been so nervous that she had completely forgotten to do her bun.

As they approached the last jump (it was more of a step really, but they were still jumping!) Molly prayed her new riding splints would hold her feet in the stirrups. She fell forward and wobbled. Everyone gasped, fearing she'd fall off, but she held on to the horn and pulled herself up straight. They just about made it over the little jump and trotted to the finish.

Molly cried: "I can ride! Yeeee-haaa!"

Odin neighed with delight as the camera flashes hurt their eyes. Ecstatic about their red first rosette, Odin celebrated with a swede and Molly hugged her parents and enjoyed squash and a barbecue with the other competitors. After their triumph, Odin returned to the stable for the rest of the week, waiting for his next lesson with Molly.

Odin and Lizzie's Adventure

Odin was thoroughly fed up with Lizzie Logger following him everywhere!

He decided to use Lizzie's adoration to his advantage. While Lizzie was annoying, she was brilliant at breaking things and escaping.

Odin explained to her that there were acres and acres of lush grass in the 'skinnies' field – the field full of lush grass, reserved for the horses and ponies that weren't overweight on other side of the village. Odin and Lizzie Logger were always kept in the 'fatties' field where there wasn't much grass. Too much grass wasn't good for ponies that were good doers in other words chubby.

Lizzie thought about her stomach even more than she thought about Odin. Her plan (Odin let her think it was her plan) meant they would be able to spend a whole day together in the 'skinnies' field. They worked out that if they could open the front gate of the stable they could make their way to the lush grazing in 'skinnies field' on the other side of the village.

When the stable was shut on Monday, Lizzie Logger (minus her cart) and Odin snuck across the yard to see if Lizzie could open the main gate. Lizzie sidled up to the gate. She pushed it and pushed it with her fat little bottom until the hinges were loose, and then, facing sideways on, she managed to lift it clean off its hinges without even breaking the string tie!

Lizzie and Odin trotted gleefully down the road until they reached the village.

They strolled lazily through the street so that they didn't look too suspicious.

The village was very exciting. They came past the post office and pub, stopped at their favourite cow parsley stop for a quick snack, and strolled past several cottages, trotting through the open garden gate of the big house to nibble the willow tree. As they munched, they saw a very angry man at the window, so hurried out of the garden with willow branches still hanging from their mouths.

Further down the street, they stopped outside Number 9 for a poo stop and then continued to Number 25. Here Odin decided to investigate the garden around the side of the house to see if there was anything delicious on the menu.

Molly was reading Pony Magazine with MTV on in the background. She could have sworn she saw a horse's bottom go past the window, with a flash of a black and white tail. She'd obviously started imagining things...

After polishing off some wild garlic, Odin and Lizzie continued through the village. Mrs Williamson lived at Number 48. Number 48 was the winning snack stop because the little old lady in her front garden offered them both a custard cream biscuit – delicious!

Leaving Mrs Williamson's, they burst through the fence by the stream and splashed through the water into the 'skinnies field' to eat until their bellies burst – that is until the owner of the stables noticed they had escaped, found them quickly and took them back.

They had a very small dinner ration that night...

Molly and Odin's Big Plan

Molly had big plans now: Pony Club camp. Who knows, maybe they'd make the Pony Club Championship or even the Paralympics one day?

She had been glued to the Paralympics, since meeting Odin, particularly the riding and the track events.

As Molly warmed Odin up for a lot of hard work in their lesson, she heard shouting coming from the indoor school: "It's not fair! Buy me a different one." It was Elspeth, refusing to ride Starlight following their defeat in the competition.

"Well, she needn't think she's riding the star of the show and she should blooming well think herself lucky that her parents were buying her a pony!" Molly grumbled under her breath.

Talk of puppies had gone quiet at Molly's house. She wondered what the chances were of her getting a larger bundle of fluff. Imagine if they were able to buy Odin! Horses probably didn't come up for sale very often, thought Molly, and certainly not stripy ones.

She was also desperate to go to Pony Club camp. This year's camp was in August and held at a large stables about 40 minutes away from where she lived and it was a week long, so everyone would be camping. Oh, she hoped her mum and dad would let her go and really hoped the riding instructor would let her take Odin. She didn't want to get stuck with a 'boring brown'. Elspeth needn't think she was palming Starlight off on her!

Their lesson turned out to be a disaster. Molly's instructor told her that the riding stable wasn't earning enough money and Odin was being sold. Molly was heartbroken. No one had told her that Odin was for sale!

She wouldn't be able to go to pony club camp, in fact, she wouldn't be able to ride at all. She needed Odin and his Western Saddle. She had actually had a nightmare a few weeks ago that someone had stolen Odin from the stable. This was worse than the nightmare where Penny and Chelsea became best friends and went off to ballet school and she was left behind – far, far worse.

She was so angry. She couldn't believe that her instructor hadn't told her and hadn't asked her family if they would like to buy Odin. Her instructor explained that Elspeth's mother had heard he was for sale and had demanded that she didn't advertise him. Elspeth's mother wouldn't take no for an answer and insisted that her daughter must have a winning pony, and she had brought the money straight over the next day.

How much could Molly earn if she helped Penny with her paper round?

When her parents arrived to pick her up, she was sobbing. Her dad said there was nothing they could do if Odin had already been sold. She was too upset to say goodbye to Odin and he wondered what he had done wrong. She always kissed him on the nose, then gave him one of those little mints with the hole in it before she left.

Odin felt sad, even though he didn't know why. The fact he was to be sold to Elspeth made Molly feel even worse. Maybe she and Elspeth could become best friends so that she could still see Odin.

Molly was so upset she couldn't eat or sleep. She actually cried at school. So did Penny – she even ran out of French sobbing. It turns out that Penny's dad was marrying his girlfriend. Penny was heartbroken. Molly was so upset about losing Odin she failed her French and maths tests at school. To be honest, she just didn't care. No Pony Club, no Paralympics.

Her mum and dad tried to console her. They promised her they would find another horse that she was able to ride, but she didn't want to ride another horse. Her mum even suggested that they visit the stable where Odin had been born to see if they could find one just like him, but she didn't want another horse. She only wanted Odin. Penny didn't want another mum either.

Her dad said that having a horse wasn't simple and they didn't have anything organised or a field or stable to keep it in and no horse box either. Why did parents put obstacles in the way of everything? It was so unfair.

She had one last lesson on Odin and felt like crying for the whole hour. It was made worse by the fact that Elspeth was watching them at the edge of the indoor school.

As Molly was helped off at the end of the lesson Elspeth said: "He'll be all mine soon. Just think, I've got the zebra horse you did your school talk on." Crumbs, how insensitive! Molly decided that she simply couldn't face school tomorrow, but her parents made her go in.

A few days later, after another dreary day of lessons, the school bus pulled up outside her house, and she made her way slowly and forlornly to her front door. Why couldn't her mum and dad do something? Your parents weren't ever supposed to let you down! She couldn't even bear to think about the fun that the rest of the Pony Club team would be having, let alone the fun Elspeth would have.

At the stable Odin had felt very uneasy all day. There had been a lot of fuss going on all around him. He had been washed and conditioned and even his hair had been plaited. He contemplated becoming famous and imagined big cameras taking photos of him and Molly, but he felt nervous as there was no sign or mention of Molly. He tried to push the flower nightmare to the back of his mind, but he felt very worried.

As he was led, gleaming, out of his stable he saw a lorry and felt even more worried. He had always longed to be a family horse, but the last time he had been put in a lorry was the day he was dressed as a flower and look what had happened to Brucie. Odin had decided he definitely didn't like lorries at all, no thank you!

When they got closer to it, he dug his hooves into the ground. Izzy the stable girl tried moving his hooves onto the ramp of the lorry, but he would not be moved. As they got him halfway up the ramp, he seized his chance and ran backwards to the bottom. Then they managed to get his front feet on to the ramp and tried to pull him up. They continued to pull him but he would not be moved.

Frightened about what the lorry meant, Odin eventually reared, raising his front feet into the air. Elspeth's mother lost her temper and started shouting: "How will they ever succeed on the competition circuit with a horse that won't load?"

As images of the flower and of Bruucie's sparkly pink halter swirled around in his head, Odin began to sweat. Elspeth's mother was red faced and sweating with temper. She marched back to her car, turned, and sped out of the car park.

As Molly approached the front door, she caught sight of a lorry parked in their front garden. It was cream with wooden trim. Oh no, don't say they were moving as well! Then she would be leaving Odin behind! She noticed the side of the lorry said 'HORSE'. A horse lorry? She was puzzled they didn't have a horse and nowhere to keep one.

Her dad met her in the porch. "Why is there a horse lorry in the drive?" she asked. Her dad said that they were going to keep looking for the perfect horse for Molly and when they found one, they would need transport. "But dad, there will never be another Odin," protested Molly.

Molly's dad told her to shush and have a look at the lorry. He said that it was old, but it even had a living area so that she wouldn't have to struggle in and out of a tent at next year's pony club camp. She tried to pretend she was excited

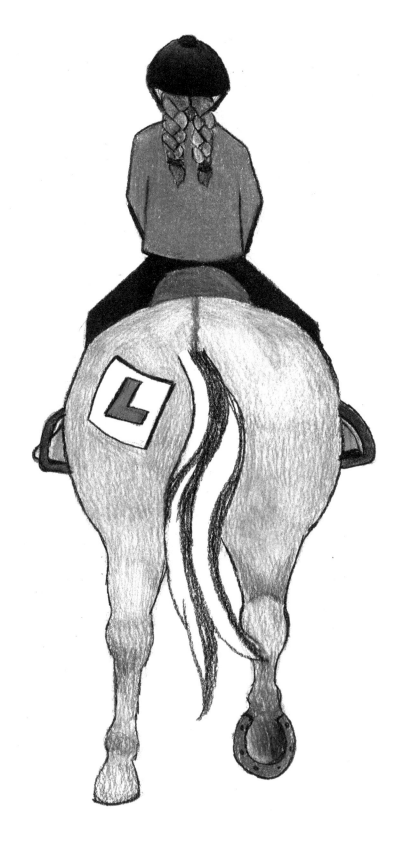

because it was so nice of them. "Come on Molly, let's check it out," said her dad. He let down the back ramp.

Oh my goodness... could she see a large bum against the rear bar? One with a black and white tail? Molly felt a surge of hope. Could it be Odin? Had her lovely dad managed to persuade the stables to let him buy her wonder horse? Her dad climbed in and turned the horse around and Molly shrieked with joy. Next to his stripy mane was a red rosette, marked 'Odin Dillon'.

In that moment, Odin decided he very much DID like lorries. If lorries brought him to Molly, he would gladly go into any lorry you liked. Dreams came true in that moment. The little Fjord horse taught Molly how to ride and she gifted him his dream of becoming a FAMILY horse. Molly and Odin taught each other not to fear being 'different' because wonderful things can happen when you are happy to stand out. If you believe in yourself, you can and you will.

9 781527 279599